About the author

Born in Birmingham in 1957, Stuart Holt was educated at Moseley Grammar School and read theology at Ridley Hall, Cambridge. For six years he worked as a teacher in schools in the UK and Germany.

He was ordained in 1987 and now works as a vicar in Hampshire and is author of *Puppets in Praise* (Harper Collins, 1993), which draws on his experience of itinerant puppet ministry. Over the past three decades his ministry has brought him into contact with many schools as a clergyman and teacher.

He has pioneered new churches, led a deanery pilgrimage to the Holy Land and is a Canon of the Diocese of Wiaswo in Ghana. His interests are writing, running, cycling, film-making and performing semi-professionally as a musician – in a group called *The Rockin' Revs*. He is married to Sally and has three grown-up children.

BEN AND THE
TIME GLOBE

Published in 2014 by Splendid Media Group (UK) Limited

Splendid Media Group (UK) Limited
The Old Hambledon Racecourse Centre
Sheardley Lane
Droxford
Hampshire
SO32 3QY
United Kingdom

www.splendidmedia.co.uk
info@splendidmedia.co.uk

British Library Cataloguing in Publication Data is available from
The British Library

978-1-909109-34-6

Commissioning Editor: Steve Clark

Jacket design and artwork by Zoe Sadler • www.zoesadler.co.uk
Internal page design by Swerve Creative • www.swerve-creative.co.uk

Printed in the UK

BEN AND THE
TIME GLOBE

STUART HOLT

For all the children who listened to and loved this story over the years and for children everywhere who love reading books.

Contents

Chapter 1
On the beach

Even as he splashed through the small rock pools idly looking for pea crabs, Ben could not escape his mother's voice. The rhythm of the sea crashing onto the rocky shore seemed to repeat her words: "Lies, lies." The "s" whispered by the tumbling shingle on the beach echoed in his mind. Temptation had got the better of him and he had raided the cake tin, but how was he supposed to know the cakes were for the old people's home? He was sure the old people would have liked him to eat the cakes anyway, old people are so kind in the realm of cake donation to children. He had denied it - another of those white lies he had a habit of telling had somehow sent his mother loopy. He fled from the house leaving her to her mutterings as she rummaged around the cupboards finding ingredients to replenish the stocks.

He had wandered down West Street, passing the steady dribble of holidaymakers heading for their hotels and B&Bs, and onto the promenade with its novelty shops and cafes catching the last of the day's trade. "Lies, lies…" The sea mocked his misdemeanour. He picked up a flatty and bounced it over the waves. He counted seven skips before it sank. He shut out the sea's mocking by covering his ears and walked on cocooned until his arms tired and he let them fall by his sides. Sitting on a convenient rock he looked out at the seascape. His mood brightened as nature soothed his hurts. He loved the sea and moving to the coast had been one big adventure. The setting sun spilled a golden pavement on the water and seagulls screeched as they battled over the flotsam of the ebbing day. The sea no longer accused, but soothed. His eyes strayed to the minutiae of the beach, limpets glued fast to the rocks with their sucker feet. Ben remembered what his teacher had taught them about the dog whelk drilling through the limpet's shell for two days after which the limpet became soup for it. He would miss Mr Field. After the holidays he would be in Miss Proud's class, but there was still four weeks until that fate so there was no need to worry just yet.

He was getting hungry, so he got up to leave but as he rose something glittering in the shingle caught his eye. He kneeled to inspect it, scraping away the pebbles he picked up the object. A crystal ball, perfectly round and smooth but not at all heavy, about 10 centimetres in diameter. It appeared to be solid glass yet lighter than a tennis ball. He held it up to the setting sun glimmering on the horizon. The light seemed to splinter into a myriad of colours, and inside the globe they whirled and mixed together.

He jumped onto the rock pretending to sword fight with imaginary opponents as they tried to take his treasure. He held the globe in front of him, once again the colours intensifying and radiating in the last glowing seconds of dusk. Then the colours flared and shone so powerfully that he dropped the globe in shock. He toppled from the rock but appeared to hang in mid-air. The sky whirled above him, the ground swayed below. His face and hands met the shingle and the colours faded into blackness.

He awoke feeling slightly sick and he shivered as though someone had walked over his grave. Getting up from the shingle he stood for a few minutes to recover. It was dark now and although he searched for the globe it eluded him. He could make out the lights on the shoreline twinkling, almost beckoning him back to reality. Stumbling over the shingle he crunched back up the beach. Breathless he reached some wooden steps leading up the small cliff to the town – steps he had never climbed. Reaching the top of the cliff he stopped in his tracks. Looking around him there was no sign of the estate which had been built that spring. No sign either of the Royal Hotel, a well-known landmark. It was so quiet. His heart was beating strongly and his throat was dry, tears welled in his eyes. Wiping them away he walked on controlling the desire to run, stifling the fear he felt. Twinkling lights grew steadily in size as he walked on. Presently he could make out the shapes of houses. The houses were old and thatched with weak yellow light barely shining through ramshackle shutters. There was no road and no street lights. Suddenly there were voices approaching, instinctively he slipped into the shadows. Two men were talking. They were dressed in faded shapeless clothes, each wore a scarf around his head and they both had beards which were spotted with dried food from the day's meals. Ben noticed one had an earring in the shape of a coiled serpent. His earlobe was partly missing and it oozed milky puss which had dried in a yellowish spot on his collar.

"I say it's better than the Valiant," shouted

the first voice. "A fine merry fight we had on our hands too, lost five good 'uns."

"Five of the best," replied the second voice. "Pigtail Pete was a fine tar, one of the best pirates that ever sailed the seas. Blown to smithereens 'e was… cannon ball through the fo'c'sle, 'ad to scrape 'is insides off the bulk'ead. I kept 'is pigtail. I runs it through my blunderbuss, it keeps the barrel nice and clean. I think he would have liked that." The pair laughed, coughed and spat green phlegm onto the door post as they entered an inn, called The Privateer.

Ben felt his heart beating quickly. These people were rough and scary and he wanted to get home. He could telephone from the inn and his dad would pick him up and it would all sort itself out. Taking a deep breath he emerged from the shadows and walked up to the door. A sudden burst of laughter startled him and panic welled up again. He sensed a movement behind him and he turned to see a huge man blocking his escape. He wore a red felt skullcap and around his large waist was a thick leather belt with a buckle made of silver fashioned into the shape of a coiled crocodile. A large curved dagger with a carved wooden handle decorated with carvings of various sizes of skull was stuffed in it. His face was tanned and his pale green eyes ice cold. A scar ran from his left ear to the edge of his nose and part of his eyelid was missing, leaving a ragged blood-red edge. His black beard hung down to his chest, under which was a faded red shirt speckled with dried multicoloured stains. He leered at Ben showing uneven brown and black teeth.

"Well, you spying little bilge rat, you want to go in? In you shall go!" The pirate's breath smelled of rotting fish and eggs. Ben had no time to explain as large rough hands grabbed his hair. The pirate opened the door and threw him inside.

Chapter 2
The Inn

Inside the inn, the air was thick with the smoke from the clay pipes and cigars that many of the customers had in their mouths. Ben's eyes watered in the murky atmosphere and his throat started to sting, and as his eyes cleared he was aware of loudly laughing people dressed in coloured garments. The pipe smokers were sitting in groups around large tables and in the various murky nooks and crannies, the clay pipes were of various lengths – they were mainly broken in some way. The pipes' original white clay had turned to various shades of brown and black as the tar and nicotine from the tobacco had seeped into them. A group in the far corner were engaged in a heated argument and a group by the log fire were singing a rude song. The room became quiet at the sight of him and Ben was aware he was being stared at. He wanted to run but a glance back at the doorway showed it to be barred by the huge pirate who had so roughly thrown him in. It was he who now spoke.

"Found the little rat spying outside, so I thought he'd like a really good look at us."

Several eyes met Ben's watery gaze. He felt afraid. Someone's voice was raised in a commanding tone from the far end of the room and the voices were stilled at his words.

"Well I think he owes us all an explanation. Now you aren't from these parts and that's obvious from your fancy rags."

Ben realised that by the "fancy rags" the man was referring to his clothes. This man now approached him. He was well dressed and cleaner than the other pirates. He sported a blue shiny jerkin, Ben thought it was made of real silk as it was similar to one of his mother's dresses. Under the jerkin he wore a red silk long sleeve doublet. The silver buttons twinkled in the light of the several oil lamps. He gave out an air of mysterious authority. Ben tried to control his trembling knees which were knocking together as he looked at him. He had shoulder-length straight white hair and large sideburns, a gold ring through his left ear quivered as he spoke. His eyes sparkled blue with life and his mouth was curved into a full warm smile. He spoke with a gentle calmness which contrasted with the raucous clamour of the other voices in the room. He had no recognisable accent.

"Allow me to introduce myself," he continued. A few laughed at this and he gave them a wink. "I am Tobias Kemp, Captain of the Black Albatross, anchored in the bay. Now lad, who are you and where do you hail from?"

Ben's story would be laughed at; perhaps they would get angry with him. He thought fast. A full minute passed before he replied.

"Please sir," he said in as confident a way as he could as he began his first lie to them. "I am not a spy, I am just a boy, and my fancy rags were bought in South America where I have been voyaging with a Captain Drake."

Captain Drake was the only name that came to his mind because of the company he was in, and unfortunately for Ben it was the worst name he could have mentioned at that particular place in time and history, as was South America. He had visited Drake's house at Buckland Abbey in Devon last week and he had learned a lot from that visit. Yet those two facts from history changed the atmosphere in the room as surely as if he had dropped a bombshell. There were several intakes of breath and mutterings in the gloom. Kemp stilled them with the raising of a hand.

"So Drake's been on the Spanish Main?" Kemp exclaimed. "The rumours seem to be true, was he plundering Spanish gold? Answer truly boy!"

"Drake has won a great victory for her majesty and has brought back much gold," Ben replied off the top of his head, the words tumbling out in a sort of old-fashioned way without him thinking. His voice was almost lost in the shouts and jeers.

The captain laughed loudly and the company joined in but then his face clouded with a frown. He got up from his seat, and although Ben reckoned him to be at least 60 years old, with great agility he leaped over the table separating them. There was a flash of steel and a knife was held to Ben's throat. The room erupted with them crying for blood.

"Now boy," Kemp hissed in his ear, "you and I are going to have a little talk."

Kemp led Ben into a back room and closed the door. "Sit!" he motioned to a small stool. Kemp towered over him, strong and menacing.

"You are a liar, boy, and a very clever one. A spy is what you are, and do not doubt that your life is now in my hands." Ben could feel the coldness of the fear creeping from inside. "Only a few know about Drake's voyage to the Spanish Main, it is a closely guarded secret. Now I happen to know that Drake sailed for Nombre de Dios but two weeks ago, the 24th of May in the year of Our Lord 1572 to be exact. You are a bold liar assuming us to be ignorant and assuming me to be a simpleton, boy. I should kill you for that alone. Tell me now what the truth is?"

"Please sir," Ben was now pleading for his life. "Please understand that the story I would tell is... so strange... it..." Ben felt sick and dizzy, the room seemed to sway, he felt confused and so tired. "I'm so tired," he sobbed, "and so confused. Please sir I am no spy. I'm just a lost boy. I came here quite by accident. I'm sorry, I want to go home, I want to go home."

Ben's sobs came long and loud, the tears streaming down his face. Kemp knew the boy was near to breaking.

"As to where you came from," Kemp said, "You will tell me in time, perhaps next week, perhaps next year, but eventually I will know. You're going to be our new cabin boy."

The door opened and Kemp left. Ben heard the key turn in the lock. He was their prisoner.

Chapter 3
At sea

Ben looked around the small room, lit by a solitary candle which cast subtle shadows into every corner. It was simply furnished with a small table and stool on which he perched nervously. There was one small window high up on the far wall, which was barred.

How strange it all seemed. He was sure he must be dreaming and pinched himself. But he didn't wake up in his familiar bed with his familiar posters of his familiar football heroes facing him on his familiar wall. He was living in this eerie, nightmare adventure. He thought of his parents, surely they would be beside themselves with worry. The police would be searching for him, his name would soon be in the newspapers, he may even be mentioned on television. How weird it was to think that there were none of those things from his time here. No television or newspapers, everything seemed so basic and stark. He was thrilled and terrified by his predicament; would he have to live out the rest of his days in this time, trapped for ever? The only way back could be through the strange Time Globe and he had no chance of finding it now, it was lying on a darkened beach. His heart was beating furiously, his senses seemed to be reeling. He was a living part of the past as though he'd jumped right into the pages of a history book. And like the words on the printed page he could not escape.

He sat alone in the gloom thinking and waiting. What was happening what would they do to him? Would they take him as their cabin boy only to murder him at sea? The sounds of merriment stabbed into the room from the party in the inn. Ben could hear songs, constant jeering and shouting. The pirates were having a good time in their particular way. Suddenly the door was unlocked and in strode a huge African man. Without speaking he placed a pewter jug of ale and a wooden platter of bread and cheese on the table. As he reached the doorway he turned and Ben noticed a deep sadness in his gaze. The man closed the door and the key turned once more in the lock. Ben was ravenous. He wolfed down the crusty bread and strong tasting cheese, the ale he supped but did not finish as there were cruddy bits of stuff in it. Weariness crept over him and he slumped over the table and fell into an uneasy sleep.

The sound of voices and a rising and falling sensation woke Ben from his uneasy dreaming. He opened his eyes and stared up into a clear starry sky. He was lying in the bottom of a rowing boat. Four large men were keeping steady time on the oars. The boat smelled of stale fruity beer and sick.

He looked down and saw both of these things slushing around in the bottom of the boat. He thought he was going to puke. He did, throwing up half-digested brown bread and mucus-slimed cheese. The back of his throat burnt with acid and beer. His eyes watered as he retched and puked up more slimy cheesy vomit. He lay in the bottom of the boat in the mess he had made. It was foul. He wept and shivered and he wanted his mum to clean him up and hold him close.

At the rear of the boat sat the black man lost in his own thoughts. A conversation was in progress between two of the oarsmen.

"Sure to be a good run this time. If I know Kemp, it's something big," said one.

"Bonecrusher Jake don't like it and you mark my words there'll be trouble in plenty this trip and no mistake," replied another. "Still I'll put my wager on Kemp any day. Bonecrusher Jake may be big alright but he ain't got no sense when it comes to plans. Remember that last raid he led, lost three men! Mind, I'm not saying I'd speak up against him – I like my liver where it is!" The men fell into laughter.

Soon the oars were shipped and Ben looked over the bow. The boat had pulled alongside a large sailing ship. The ship had three tall masts and a number of cannons. It was black like a floating shadow on the water. At the top of the middle mast flew a black flag and painted on the stern in gold letters was the name Black Albatross.

Large rough hands lifted him whilst other hands reached down from the darkness and pulled him aboard. Ben now stood on the deck of the pirate ship and looked around. The pirates were going about their various tasks and the darkened ship was a hive of activity. Captain Kemp and Bonecrusher Jake stood on the bridge shouting orders in sharp rasping tones, which the crew immediately obeyed.

"So you're the new cabin boy are you lad?" Ben turned to face the one who addressed him. A portly man dressed in a black leather jerkin was looking at him. His hair was thick and grey, he was tanned and wrinkled. He only had one leg, the other missing from the knee. The bottom half of this leg was made of a wooden peg which was highly polished and glinted in the lamplight. "Peg-leg's me name lad and I'm your only friend, protector and instructor for the time being, so you'd better come with me below."

Without hesitation Ben followed the hobbling figure. His progress was remarkably quick and as he walked his false leg clicked rhythmically on the planking.

They made their way aft and descended a steep stairway to a cabin which Ben at once realised was the galley. Pots and pans hung from a huge stove which stood at its centre. There was a delicious smell of stew which mingled with the musty air.

"This here is the galley, my galley. I'm chief cook and bottle washer and you're to help me prepare the vittles for this scum who sail the seas. If you do wrong I'll beat you hard, if you do as you're told I'll treat you decent.

Understand boy?" Ben nodded. "Now go over there and wash all that mess off. You smell like death breath!"

So this was to be his life from now on, a slave to the pirates, fetching, cleaning, carrying, all the miserable jobs he'd always avoided doing at home. These were now his responsibility for how long? For ever, perhaps. The one-legged pirate put Ben to work polishing pans. The work was hard and before long his hand ached. The pirate stirred a large pot simmering on the stove, which began to fill the galley with a wonderful aroma of herbs and spices reminding Ben of his mother's home-cooked Irish stew. He thought of her and a tear rolled slowly down his cheek. He quickly wiped it away.

The ship began to rock gently from side to side and Ben realised that they had set sail. They were sailing away into the darkness, away from home into the unknown.

Chapter 4
King Death

The days passed and on they sailed, aided by a strong south-easterly wind which carried them speedily on their voyage. Ben had thrown up twice more; once into the dinner he was preparing, which he stirred into it before he got into trouble, and the other time over the side of the ship. He had chosen the wrong side and the wind blew his spew back all over him. He had to be washed down with sea water. He worked hard and Peg-leg rewarded him with food and the occasional kind word.

He spent most of his time in the galley, afraid to venture onto the decks as he feared the pirates and especially the one called Bonecrusher Jake, who had so roughly thrown him into the inn on the night he travelled back in time. He learnt that he got his fearful name because once in a fight it was said that he killed three armed men by crushing their skulls with his bare hands. On the occasions when he did have to go above to throw rubbish overboard and just to breath fresh air, he was aware of Bonecrusher Jake's hardened stare, the man terrified Ben and he kept well out of his way.

Ben soon became familiar with the pirates likes and dislikes as his duties involved serving their food, and he came to recognise each one's importance. There seemed to be a chain of command and the first mate was a Frenchman by the name of Lamballe. He was a small man with a sly grin, Ben thought he looked a little like a weasel. He smiled a lot and said little, and seemed fairly pleasant compared to the others. He spent long hours talking to Captain Kemp in hushed tones, and as he did so Ben noticed that Bonecrusher Jake watched the two with malice. Ben had learned that the silent African was named Mabu. He did not eat with the other pirates but alone in the bows of the ship where he slept. Peg-leg took his food to him and seemed to spend long periods with the sad and silent man.

Most of the crew were noisy, ignorant men with few table manners. They ate their food often complaining and cursing and seemed to disgust the captain at times. He would shout for silence when the noise became unbearable to him. Kemp behaved impeccably at the table and had obviously learned his manners in different company to his bawdy crew. The men seemed to respect the captain on the whole, but Ben was aware of some general ill feeling when Kemp would leave the table to talk with Lamballe in his cabin.

One night, as Ben lay in his hammock that was strung up in the galley, he heard hushed talk outside the door. Peg-leg was snoring as usual and this made it difficult for Ben to hear what was being said. By the tone of the conversation, Ben sensed a secret was being shared which aroused his curiosity. Quietly he slipped to the deck and crept across the galley to the door. He peeped through the crack between the planks. Bonecrusher Jake and four other pirates were deep in conversation.

"We're agreed then," said Bonecrusher Jake. "Three days time at night when all's quiet and there's little chance of a fight we'll do it quick."

"Slit their gizzards before they have a chance to wake up," replied a particularly gruesome pirate by the name of Hookhand Ned drawing the hook which replaced his left hand across his throat and smiling.

"And we split fair shares," he added.

"Aye," whispered Bonecrusher Jake, "But

the ruby's mine and if any of you lay so much as a finger on it you can wave goodbye to that finger along with your miserable liver."

Just at that moment a rat scuttled from its hiding place in search of crumbs. The movement startled Ben and he let out a cry. The pirates stopped their conspiratorial conversation and looked towards the galley. The door was flung open and once more Ben was face to face with the evil pirate. The others melted into the darkness. Ben backed away as Bonecrusher Jake advanced towards him, grim-faced and determined to do him harm. A knife blade glistened in the moonlight. The pirate was on him in an instant and cupped his hand to Ben's mouth. Ben struggled and kicked, fighting for his life. Peg-leg grunted in his sleep and continued to snore. Ben felt the cold steel at his throat and the needle like stab of pain as the point pierced his neck. Hookhand Ned appeared at the door.

"Kemp's roaming about," he hissed. "Leave the boy be!"

The huge man hesitated as Ben's life hung in the balance. There was a long pause where it seemed the air could have been cut with the knife at his throat.

"Not this way," said Hookhand Ned, "Too risky."

"Right, bilge rat," whispered the pirate into Ben's face, his breath smelled of rotten cabbage. "One word, just one word to anyone and you're dead, understand?"

Ben nodded. The pirate slowly released his grip and giving Ben one last stare, which froze his blood, he left as silently as he had entered. Ben breathed hard – he had survived this time, but for how long? How long before Bonecrusher Jake picked his moment and decided the time was right to finish him off? His life was now very much in danger.

Ben spent the next morning in a state of delayed shock, but he was too terrified to tell anyone. Peg-leg moaned about his poor preparation of the vegetables, and asked awkward questions about the small cut on his neck. Ben passed this off with the explanation that he had fallen on the slippery deck. He knew that he dare not tell even this kindly pirate of his ordeal in the dark, such was the fear that Bonecrusher Jake had instilled in him.

Ben served the breakfast that morning, cautiously avoiding the evil pirate who had so nearly murdered him in the night. His cold stare turned his knees to jelly and made his heart beat fast. The pirates finished their breakfast and went off about their daily tasks. As he washed up he wondered what Bonecrusher Jake was going to do, what was the ruby he had talked of? He was taken from his thoughts by Peg-leg asking for Mabu's breakfast. As he spooned out the gruel he asked another question that had been puzzling him.

"Why does Mabu eat on his own, and why doesn't he talk, can't he speak English?"

"I wondered when you'd ask that," replied Peg-leg. "He eats on his own because he's a slave and isn't fit to eat with the rest of the crew. He don't talk 'cos he ain't got no tongue, and he can't hear what you say neither. Once he was involved in a fight with one of the crew over some beads he wore. The crewman wanted 'em and Mabu wasn't going to let him take them. He hit the man just once and killed him outright. Now that ain't right for a slave and his punishment fitted the crime. Kemp cut out his tongue so he couldn't argue no more, and he punctured his ears so he couldn't hear what they said about him. He's here to serve and is treated badly by all. If he so much as raises a finger to any of the crew for whatever reason he's under pain of death, and that was the last thing he heard anyone say to him in this world. I takes pity on him and feeds him better than most know."

As Ben heard this story he was filled with pity for this poor man, and the story made him even more fearful for his own safety. After all, Ben was also a slave.

That night Ben was so worried he couldn't sleep, for he knew that Bonecrusher Jake had planned for something bad to happen in three days, and one of those days had now ended. He had two days left to make a decision, the most important decision of his life.

As he lay in his rocking hammock he heard them singing their sea shanties late into the night…

*King Death is our captain his banner
we fly,*
*King Death is our master surrender
or die!*
*Load up the falconer cannon and
blast,*
*Steady your aim boys and bring down
her mast!*
*King Death is our captain his banner
we fly,*
*King Death is our master surrender
or die!*

Chapter 5
Surprise visitors

The next day brought a strong wind and high seas. Grey skies loomed over the Black Albatross, which pitched in the foaming waves. There was talk of an oncoming storm and the captain gave orders for the ship to be made ready. Large objects were lashed and the sails were shortened. The Pirate's flag 'The banner of King Death' was lowered and stowed away. Ben was impressed with the efficiency of the pirate crew, who worked well together, each man knowing his task and following Kemp's orders. Ben was also given a task, he was ordered by Lamballe to the front of the ship to assist Mabu.

Ben found Mabu sitting cross-legged surrounded by weapons and ammunition. He was cleaning a musket, lost in his own thoughts. He sensed Ben's arrival and motioned for him to sit down. Ben did so and for some moments the two stared at each other. Ben was immediately aware of Mabu's piercing eyes, his eyes seemed to stand out from his face in the gloom and showed so much suffering. Yet Ben could see that they were keen and sparkling. The rest of Mabu's face bore the same solemn expression. Ben smiled nervously not knowing how to communicate with the stone-like man.

Mabu's face creased into a vague glimmer of a smile, as though it was something he once did well, but had forgotten. His lips parted to reveal strong white teeth and for a moment the smile reached the eyes and then as quickly as it had appeared it vanished leaving the same blank stare.

"Mabu", said Ben breaking the silence, "I

am here to help you clean the weapons."

Mabu understood and passed over a cutlass and a rag. Ben began to polish the tarnished blade and Mabu continued to clean the musket which Ben believed to be a blunderbuss. The two worked on in silence as the ship continued to heave in the swell. Mabu was reluctant to look Ben in the eye and Ben wanted to ask him so many questions: where did he come from? How did he join the crew?

Ben continued polishing and then jumped back involuntarily as the silent man touched his arm. Mabu smiled and let out a deep chuckling sound from low in his throat. Then Ben also saw the funny side of the situation and laughed too. It had seemed so long since he had laughed, and he wondered if it was the same in Mabu's case. Any fears he may have had about this unusual man vanished at that moment and the two were destined to become firm friends.

"Can you understand me?" Ben asked.

Mabu nodded touching his lips and then his eyes. "You can lip read?" Ben said. Mabu smiled and nodded. Reaching behind him he handed Ben a pewter goblet in which was a fair quantity of rum, he motioned for Ben to drink. Ben knew he shouldn't do this normally. The liquid burnt Ben's throat, setting his belly on fire and he had to show great self-control to stop choking. He passed the drink back and realised that the gesture of friendship in this time of history had been rightly received. "Do you know where we're going?" Ben enquired.

Mabu nodded again and beckoned Ben over to him. He picked up a piece of sackcloth in which was a slate with a small piece of lead. On this he drew a shape which seemed to resemble the continent of South America. How did Mabu know how to draw maps? Ben wondered. Mabu pointed to his own eyes and then to the rear of the ship. Ben was puzzled, he frowned, Mabu wrote a word 'Drake'. He then did something which made Ben's flesh creep, he drew his finger across his throat.

"Kill Drake?" Ben exclaimed.

Mabu slowly nodded. He then pointed to his

own eyes, to Ben's lips and again to the rear of the ship.

"You've seen people talking?" Ben asked, and Mabu nodded. Perhaps it is Kemp, Ben thought.

"You've seen Kemp talking to the Frenchman, Lamballe?" he guessed. Mabu nodded furiously. "You have read their lips and seen maps?" Mabu nodded once more. He was obviously pleased with the conversation they were having. Ben whistled as these facts were taken in. Surely Kemp and Lamballe had not even guessed that Mabu would gain knowledge of their plot as he served in the captain's cabin. What a perfect spy he was.

Any further questions would have to wait as the door opened and Hookhand Ned shouted, "All hands on deck, quick!"

The two conspiratorial companions went up as ordered, the pirate taking pleasure in kicking them both as they climbed up. Many of the crew were gazing intently to starboard and Kemp stood on the bridge peering through an eye glass. From the excited chatter of the crew Ben heard that a small rowing boat had been spotted. He joined the pirates, straining his eyes for a glimpse of it. He could see the small boat battling in the heaving sea. As the ship drew nearer he could make out three figures, one was a man standing at the prow, waving and shouting. As the Black Albatross was not flying the pirate flag, the crew of the rowing boat didn't know that they were approaching a pirate ship. Ben knew he had no way of warning the three occupants of the boat, so along with the rest he awaited their arrival. Soon the boat came alongside and the three occupants were clearly visible. One was a lean, tall, suntanned man, another an older man who was rather plump and it was he who was rowing. The third occupant – the one who had waved to them – was no more than a boy of Ben's age. All three were shabbily dressed and much the worse for wear. They all had to be lifted out of the boat and soon they were standing rather shakily on the deck of the Black Albatross.

Kemp descended from the bridge and showing no sympathy for the three castaways condition, immediately began to question them. Who were they and how did they come to be adrift in an open boat so far from land? It was the tall man who spoke, the other two standing behind him looking uneasy.

"My name is Mortimer, Captain Mortimer of the merchant vessel Solway. We were on a voyage transporting spices to Dartmouth when there was an uprising, a mutiny on the ship. The first mate started it, cast us off: me, my cabin boy and my cook." He motioned to his companions then fell to his knees as he was so weakened from the ordeal. His companions helped him to his feet.

"Please sir," spoke the old man, "we've not eaten or drunk for two days and I think the captain is delirious, he's been strange all day. Could we beg some food and drink before we answer any more questions?"

Kemp thought for a moment then pulled himself up to his full height to achieve a commanding air. "You're on a pirate ship, if you eat and drink with us you become our slaves, you ask no questions you only speak when spoken to, break these rules, you die." The three nodded and were taken below decks. "Peg-leg, boy, feed them!" ordered Kemp.

He then gave orders for the course to be changed and the crew went back to their duties chatting about the incident and all the work that their new slaves could do for them. Bonecrusher Jake was thinking deeply and his eyes narrowed as he went below decks. Four of the pirates followed him.

Chapter 6
Slaves on a pirate ship

Peg-leg and Ben attended to the castaways and fed them on ship's biscuits and water – it was all they could manage after their ordeal.

Ben found the three well-mannered and pleasant new company. It was good to have someone his own age to talk to although they had little in common. Sebastian would tell him tales of sea adventures he had experienced as a cabin boy. They were all obviously delighted to be alive and although the work they had to do for the pirates was hard and horrible Mortimer remarked that it was better to be a slave on a pirate ship than food for the fish, as they most certainly would have been had they remained on the small boat with nothing to drink.

The old man unnerved Ben somewhat as he seemed to look at him with deeply questioning glances at times. This went on until at last he asked a question.

"Those are strange clothes you're wearing lad, where did you come by them?" Ben gave the reply that had satisfied the pirates that they came from South America where he had voyaged. But the old man replied," I thought I heard you say to young Sebastian that you were picked up in England by the pirates."

"Yes that is the truth," Ben replied, "but I forgot to mention that I had previously voyaged in South America."

The old man stared for some moments at Ben, deep in thought, during which Ben felt strangely nervous. Then his face broke into a smile. "I see," he remarked and the matter was dropped from the conversation.

It appeared from the story that the three told

that the mutiny had been rather a peaceful one. The first mate of the Solway had all of the crew behind him and the ship was taken without a shot being fired. Mortimer believed that the crew had been primed from the outset so nothing could be done to resist. The old man, whose name was James, and the boy Sebastian remained loyal to the captain throughout so all three were set adrift, the crew jeering and waving as they sailed away. The only provisions allowed them were one jug of water and one loaf of bread. This had run out after two days and they had gone a further two days with nothing all. They were indeed lucky to be alive. All three said that they would like to rest and Peg-leg in his thoughtful way provided comfortable bedding, even though it was infested with weevils.

The galley door opened as they were bunking down and a pirate called One Eye explained that he had been sent to guard the new arrivals to ensure that they behaved themselves. Ben was dismissed and decided to go and talk to Mabu again. He found Mabu busy scrubbing the decks, so collecting a scrubbing brush he set about helping him. As their heads met, Mabu again in his unique way told Ben the rest of what he wanted to know. He motioned with his head to Bonecrusher Jake's cabin and then to Kemp's, then again he drew his finger across his throat.

"Bonecrusher Jake means to kill Kemp?" asked Ben.

Mabu nodded and then quickly looked away as a pirate approached, he was staggering slightly and smelt of rum. His name was Sneaky Sanchez. Ben and Mabu continued scrubbing in silence. The bucket they were using was kicked over, the pirate laughed cruelly and as Mabu attempted to pick it up the pirate kicked him hard in the face. Mabu hardly flinched as blood trickled from his nose, but stared coldly at the man. Ben felt the anger rising within. How dare he treat Mabu like this? He rose to his feet anger blazing in his eyes and his fists clenched.

The pirate turned towards him, "Well?" he

said still laughing. "What are you going to do to protect your dumb friend?" Ben threw himself at the pirate, but the man anticipated his move and side stepped tottering slightly. Ben sprawled on the deck. The pirate lifted his foot in an attempt to kick Ben also, but in a flash Mabu caught his foot and brought him down heavily. The pirate cursed loudly and then started to whimper as Mabu towered above him.

"Mabu he go mad! Mabu he go mad!" the pirate shouted loudly. "Help! Murder!"

Mabu stared coldly unmoving then looked around with fear as the pirate continued his shouting. A door was flung open and out came three pirates armed and ready for action. Ben looked on horror stricken as Mabu, seeing no escape, began to climb the rigging. Driven by fear he climbed until he was high up the mast, he looked down his white eyes bulging out of his dark face which was a mask of terror. Without warning a shot rang out – one of the pirates had drawn a pistol. Mabu hung for a moment on the rigging then he lost his footing.

Ben prayed for invisible hands to hold him but it was not to be, he was falling, falling, turning and twisting as he came down landing in the rolling sea. The crew rushed to the rail, jostling for position, waiting for the man to surface, but he did not. Kemp appeared, and after the crew had explained what had happened they were ordered below.

Ben wept, tears stinging his eyes and sobs cleaving his throat. He ran to the galley and buried his face in Peg-leg's shoulder.

"Mabu's dead," he sobbed. "Mabu's dead and it's all my fault, all my fault, I wish I'd never come, I wish I was at home."

Peg-leg comforted him as best he could as did the castaways, but Ben felt a sadness so heavy it seemed to break his heart. This was the worst day of his life, if only he hadn't picked up that globe, if only he hadn't stolen the cakes. If only he could bring Mabu back but there was nothing he could do, and Ben knew for the first time the feeling adults call despair.

That night brought a great storm, as though a

higher hand was showing outrage at the murder. The ship rolled heavily in the mountainous seas. Ben slept fitfully with fearful dreams of the drama he had witnessed: Mabu falling, falling. The morning brought a lull and the ship was inspected for damage. The only loss was the castaway's boat which had broken free in the storm. This didn't worry the castaways who agreed they would be glad not to see it again as it reminded them of their ordeal.

Ben felt like death warmed up as he served the pirates their breakfast. Bonecrusher Jake was late, as were several others of the crew. If the evil pirate's plans had not changed, then today he would do as Mabu had said, he would kill Captain Kemp, take command of the ship and Ben's fate would be sealed.

Chapter 7
A secret shared

Ben's job had changed since the arrival of the castaways. Sebastian helped out in the galley, so Ben found himself spending more time scrubbing decks as Mabu had done. This work was more tiring and his knees were reddened by the deck boards, but it allowed him fresh air and he could keep an eye on Bonecrusher Jake and his gang, so that when something did happen he would have a chance to escape over the side and take his chances in the sea.

James was the oldest castaway and he was

ordered to help Ben this day, so they scrubbed the deck together. The morning was bright and sunny and a strong breeze carried the Black Albatross along. As they worked in silence Ben turned over plans and schemes until his head ached. He knew that he must do something to warn Kemp, but even if he did would Kemp believe him? There was going to be a bloodbath of a fight surely and most of the crew seemed to be with Bonecrusher Jake. Ben again thought of his desperate escape plan. He was a strong swimmer but not strong enough to stay alive at sea for more than a few hours. He was after all a boy out of time with no real friends on the ship, so who could help him? He had made friends of sorts with Sebastian but he saw little of him as their duties kept them apart. Mortimer was still weak from his ordeal and would be of little help in a skirmish. Ben's thoughts turned to the old man silently scrubbing the deck by his side. Perhaps he could help if Ben told him of the plot, but what use would an old man and a boy be against so many hardened pirates? The situation was hopeless – he had to keep his wits about him and be ready to jump overboard. Yet perhaps he had some special power which he had not yet discovered, after all he was a time traveller from the future. He knew things that they did not, but he had no weapons which he could use from his own time. If he just had a box of matches he could start a fire as a diversion, but he had nothing.

The old man was whistling a tune to himself as he worked. Ben recognised the tune from somewhere and joined in as the two worked steadily. Lunchtime was spent eating salted meat brought up from the galley by Sebastian. Ben and James sat together on the deck shaded by one of the mizzen sails. It was the old man who struck up conversation.

"You don't say much Ben, I've got a feeling something is troubling you, do you want to tell me about it? Perhaps an old head can offer some advice."

"I don't think that you could help," Ben replied. "But thanks for the offer."

"I may be able to help more than you think Ben, if you'd just tell me the facts."

Ben thought for a moment, it might be alright to tell him something just to get some of it off his chest. So Ben started to talk, he talked about his capture in the inn, of how he was forced to work for the pirates. He told of Bonecrusher Jake's plan to take the Black Albatross and of the terrifying night when he was nearly murdered, of Mabu spying then learning of Kemp and Lamballe's plan to kill Drake and of the ruby that Bonecrusher Jake meant to steal from Kemp. Finally he told him that the pirates meant to take the ship that very night and there was nothing that they could do to save themselves.

The old man listened intently nodding now and again during the story and asking for further details on one or two points. When Ben had finished he paused for a time deep in thought.

"Well," he said at last." That is a very interesting story, but are you sure that you have told me everything?"

"Yes," Ben replied, "why?"

"Well," James replied, looking at him questioningly from beneath his bushy eyebrows. "I don't believe that you've told me all of how you came to find the pirates, it has some weak points. Let's go back to the inn, perhaps you'd like to tell me some more about that?"

"It was full of noisy pirates singing," Ben exclaimed. "And it was frightening."

"No!" interrupted the old man. "Before you entered the inn, let's say one hour before, where were you then? Where were you going? Which town did you come from?"

"Seaford," Ben replied quickly.

"I've never been there," James said, "what is it like?"

"It's very pretty", Ben said. Suddenly Ben thought back to his home town, the town he had grown to love in the short time he had lived there. How far he was now from that town, how long had he been away? "It's beautiful James, I wish you could have seen it. It has a lovely promenade and you can watch the boats going in and out of the harbour. At night the lights reflect in the water all colours. That's when it is at its best at night. They put up coloured lights."

"Thank you," James said. "Well it's back to work now."

They continued the deck scrubbing in the heat of the afternoon and it became hot and unpleasant work. They again whistled tunes together. Ben remembered some of them and began to sing one and the old man joined in. "*I am sailing, I am sailing, home again across the sea, I am sailing, stormy waters, to be near you, to be free.*" Then like a bolt from the blue it struck Ben that the song was from his own time, it hadn't been written in 1572! Ben stared open mouthed at James, the old man who now looked at him and he was smiling.

"Allow me to introduce myself properly," he said. "My full name is Professor James Brent, Head of Geology at the University of Southampton. I am like you a traveller in time, as I come from the year 1999."

For the first time in his life Ben fainted.

Chapter 8
Mutiny

Ben awoke and was surprised to find himself lying in his hammock. He looked around and saw the old man sitting on a chair beside him.

"How are you feeling?" James asked.

"Sort of shaky," Ben replied, then he burst into tears of relief or happiness – he didn't know what kind they were, but with each sob pebbles of heaviness seemed to lift from his heart. James put a reassuring hand on his shoulder as he let out the feelings.

He passed Ben a crumpled tissue. "My

last Kleenex," he smirked. "I'm sorry to have given you such a shock but I had to be sure that you were also from the future. Your clothes of course alerted me as soon as I set eyes on you, but you see you could have found them or stolen them. With all that you've been through my revelation about myself just tipped the balance of your mind and I was very concerned at what I'd done."

Ben dried his face and raised himself on one arm. "I just can't seem to take it all in," he said.

"I think you'd best tell me your entire story now Ben, there is so much I need to know and it will help you to talk openly, here drink this." James passed him a bowl of broth which Ben wolfed down. As he did so it seemed that the moments they were sharing had a quality of unearthly magic. Here they were, both travellers out of their own times, James from 1999 and Ben from the 21st century, both of them from a world of technology, motor cars, fast trains and aeroplanes. Things which they used every day and took for granted in their own times were not heard of here in 1572. Yet in this time they shared danger with the pirate crew. The only division between them was time, the ever-continuing stream of change. As surely as the earth revolved around the sun, time would never stop bringing with it new ideas, new inventions and new hopes for the future.

Ben explained his walk along the beach and how he discovered the Time Globe, his experience of the swirling colours, how he had suddenly found himself thrown back and his capture at the hands of Bonecrusher Jake. As he spoke James nodded excitedly.

"This globe Ben was it about the size of a tennis ball?" Ben nodded. "And what was the exact date on which you held it up to the sun?"

"It was 27th July,' Ben replied. "I know that for sure."

"That is most relevant," James said

thoughtfully. "Now I think I should tell you my tale." Ben settled back to listen.

"As I told you before I am Professor James Brent, head of Geology at Southampton University. I enjoy my work and still have a great interest in rocks, particularly in searching for new kinds. I was researching a particular type of mineral that could be used for high stress applications. Whenever I get the time I like to go out into the field looking for samples to aid my research. I get a great deal of pleasure in chiselling lumps out of rock faces. There were some caves that I particularly wanted to explore down in Devon, so I decided to take a week's holiday down there and mix business with pleasure. I booked in at a B&B in Dartmouth which provided for my simple wants, and the proprietor didn't mind me coming back often muddy at the oddest of hours. I often worked late into the evening, eating alone when I returned. One day the exact date was 27th July 1999 and I was working in a cave when

I came upon a strange globe shaped rock set into the rock face. I removed it carefully; triumphant at my discovery I carried it out of the cave and onto the seashore. It fascinated me. It was evening I remember and there was a beautiful sunset. I held the globe up to the sun and then I experienced the same sensation of dizziness. When I awoke I discovered that I had been transported back in time. Survival was my first instinct and in a daze I staggered up the beach leaving the globe behind me. I managed to procure some clothes befitting to the time I was in and returned to the beach many times when I had collected my thoughts, but I could not find the globe. I supposed that it had been washed out to sea. I got a job helping a fisherman in the village for my keep and worked for him for six months learning basic seamanship and how to mend nets. Unfortunately he found that he could no longer keep me and so I had to find another job. To eat you need money and to get money you need to work.

So I signed up on a ship sailing for South America – the Solway. The work was hard but interesting and Captain Mortimer was a kind man, but weak-willed and prone to drink too much. One night the crew carried out their mutiny and the rest you know."

Ben found the old man's tale fascinating and the two agreed that perhaps by some higher hand of destiny the globe had been carried by the currents to be washed up at Seaford for Ben to find. The old man looked long and hard at Ben before speaking again.

"I believe," he said, "that we have been sent here for a purpose, for whatever reason our presence here may have already changed in some way the future of certain people. We must be careful not to interfere in a way that would deliberately cause harm. We know that this ship is on an errand which cannot succeed because, as we know through history, Drake was victorious in the South Pacific and not killed by pirates. This ship is going to fail in its mission to kill Drake, perhaps though we will have a part to play."

Ben shuddered to think that somehow by some irresponsible act they could change the future. Their best course of action was to do nothing, to keep their heads down and wait, but they both knew that this was impossible as their instinct to survive would cause them to act. Their conversation was interrupted by the sound of gunfire, shouts and the clashing of swords. Bonecrusher Jake had started the mutiny!

Chapter 9
Fight to the death

Ben and James quickly moved to the door and partly opened it so that they could witness the fight for the control of the Black Albatross. In the evening light the pirates could be seen skirmishing. Bonecrusher Jake and his followers were grouping at the front of the ship. The bloodthirsty pirate stood on the fo'c'sle shouting orders to his gang. He held a smouldering blunderbuss in one hand and a blood-smeared cutlass in the other. At his feet lay a badly wounded pirate, a red stain covering his left shoulder. Sneaky Sanchez was in the thick of the fight, cutting down man after man as he wildly slashed with his cutlass.

Cutthroat Cortez climbed the rigging and, aiming his blunderbuss, fired into the seething mass of fighting pirates. One man fell to the ground, killed instantly as the bullet passed through his heart. Kemp and Lamballe stood at the rear of the ship. Kemp held two blunderbusses and waved them frantically around, letting off both at once into an advancing mutineer. Lamballe was engaged in a cutlass duel with Hookhand Ned. He fought furiously, steel met steel again and again but he didn't have the build to properly defend himself. With a final thrust his adversary ran him through, he sank to his knees and, uttering something in French, died where he fell, still kneeling.

Kemp and his followers were pushed further and further back until they were cornered on the bridge. Kemp looked at the overwhelming odds and suddenly dropped both pistols and raised his hands in surrender. The remnants of his loyal crew, now numbering 4 against

Bonecrusher Jake's 12, followed his example and dropped their weapons. The mutiny was completed.

Ben and James watched hearts pounding as Bonecrusher Jake descended to the main deck. Swaggering, he climbed the steps which led up to the bridge and faced Kemp.

"You know what I want," he said. "Give it to me."

Kemp handed over a bag. Bonecrusher Jake opened it and held in his hand a ruby the size of a golf ball. Mortimer, who had been a sick man since arriving on board the Black Albatross, stood on the main deck watching wide-eyed. He seemed to be mumbling incoherently to himself, and then defiantly he faced the bridge.

"No!" he shouted. "You will never take my ship! The Solway is mine: no mutineer will ever sail in her."

Before anyone could act he leaped up into the fo'c'sle. Ben and James rushed out of the galley hoping to stop him, but it was too late. Mortimer opened the door to the powder room and taking a flint in his hand he struck it. It sparked – the explosion was deafening. Splinters of wood flew in all directions, shards of metal tore into the sails and embedded themselves in the masts. Everyone fell flat on their faces. Confusion and panic arose as the ship heaved and swayed, shuddered and shook. Smoked belched from the prow, flames licked up the mast and sails. The ship's timbers cracked and sparks flew high into the evening sky. The Black Albatross suddenly listed to starboard and waves broke over the deck. Pirates were running and jumping overboard as the ship floundered and started to sink.

Bonecrusher Jake lurched forward and fell onto the bridge rail. The ruby he had been jealously clutching fell from his hand onto the deck below. It rolled straight into Ben's hand. Ben's eyes met those of the pirate and murder flared in them. Ben and James reacted immediately, throwing themselves over the port rail. Sticking closely together they swam as fast as they could away from the burning, dying ship. When they were a safe distance away they looked back to see the stern slowly slipping beneath the waves. There were shouts and cries for help as the pirates desperately searched for pieces of flotsam to hold on to. They stared for some minutes, treading water about 50 metres from the scene. Ben counted three heads bobbing in the water.

Bonecrusher Jake, as far as he could make out, was not among them.

They knew that they must put as much distance as possible between themselves and the surviving pirates. Turning they struck out and keeping a steady pace swam for a good 30 minutes. They could no longer hear the cries for help. Stopping, they removed their trousers, tied knots in the legs and inflated them. Holding onto these as life savers they floated in the water. They both realised that survival was only possible for a short while, soon the gripping numbness of exposure would paralyse their limbs. But they had the instinct to live and intended to hold on until the last moment.

They floated like this for some time until

they no longer knew how long they had been in the water. They spoke little and held hands to keep together, saving their energy. Ben looked up at the stars and the full moon which gave the water a silvery sheet.

He could no longer feel his legs and nausea took hold of him. Waves were beginning to break over his head. If only he had not taken those cakes and had just walked along the beach.

"I'm sorry Mum," he cried. "I'm sorry."

A shadowy hand filled his vision; the hand of death had come to claim him.

Chapter 10
A friend found

The first thing that Ben was aware of when he recovered consciousness was that he had a hard round object in his left pocket and that he was lying in the bottom of a boat. His vision swam for a moment and then cleared. He looked up to see The Professor smiling down on him, his face framed by a bright blue sky. The Professor raised Ben's head and put a rag soaked in water to his lips. Ben sucked on this and quenched his thirst. Looking round, he realised that they were not the only occupants of the boat. Sitting in the prow was someone he never thought he'd see again, his strong white teeth flashing a warm smile.

"Mabu!" Ben exclaimed. "You're alive... or are we all dead?"

"No we're not all dead," laughed The Professor. "Although we feared for your life Ben. I must admit that it was touch and go and we both owe our lives to Mabu. His quick action after he picked us up certainly saved us."

"But what happened?" asked Ben, sitting up. "We were sure that he had drowned."

"From what he has explained to me in signs," The Professor replied, "after falling from the rigging he swam under the Black Albatross and held onto the Solway's life boat. Keeping out of sight until nightfall, he freed the boat and escaped. We of course believed that the boat had been lost in the storm, so no one knew."

"How long have we been in the boat?" Ben asked.

"It's now around 3 o'clock in the afternoon and you have slept for a good 14 hours, sometimes calling out. You seemed to be very worried about those cakes," The Professor replied smiling kindly.

Looking around the boat, Ben could see that they were well provided for. A tarpaulin was strung across the stern which contained a good supply of rain water. There were several fish of various sizes and types which would keep them going for some days, although The Professor explained that they would have to eat them raw if they were hungry.

"What are our plans now?" asked Ben, who was wondering which course they would take if any.

"We'll just have to trust to luck. When Mabu last spied on Kemp, he learned that we were about four hundred miles off the coast of South America. There is no land near and so we can expect to remain at sea for some time, yet we must look for any passing vessel and keep a round the clock watch. Obviously our water and food must be used sparingly so it is not going to be a pleasant voyage I'm afraid. The main cause for concern is a storm, but God willing we may yet prevail. Mabu is taking this watch and I will take the next. When you feel up to it you can take your turn."

They spent the rest of the day conserving their energy and telling tales and jokes to pass the time. Ben was fascinated by the huge ruby which had come into his possession and imagined it to be worth a small fortune. He handed it to the others to inspect, but Mabu wouldn't touch it as he believed it to be unlucky because so many had desired it. The Professor gave them a short lecture on how it was made and how valuable it was. However the value for him lay in its geological interest.

"How this stone would help my research at the university," The Professor mused. "I could give the lecture of my life. This ruby originates from Burma – it is of the highest quality."

"Then you must keep it," said Ben. "And if we by some chance get back to our own time I would feel that some good has come out of all of this." The Professor tried to refuse but Ben knew that this one man would use the ruby for the good of others and not for personal greed, so the matter was settled.

After some days Ben had sufficiently recovered to take his first watch. He rather enjoyed this at first, but found that after two or three hours scanning the horizon with the others asleep it became very monotonous. Once he thought he saw an object on the horizon but is disappeared. They drifted for what seemed like weeks catching fish and water to stay alive. Morale dropped and they felt like prisoners incarcerated in a floating cell. They took the occasional swim and Mabu would perform tricks, disappearing for minutes before he bobbed up on the other side of the boat and surprised them. Once they saw a group of dolphins which swam up to the boat and circled it curiously. Ben threw them a fish and was delighted by their antics. He decided that if he ever got back to school he would find out more about these wonderful animals.

Then one day came the long awaited sighting of a ship. It was Mabu who first spotted the speck on the horizon. The heavy oars were put into the rowlocks and they set off towards it. They could hardly contain their excitement as the distance between the two boats narrowed and they could make out the masts. The three of them stood up waving frantically and shouted for a long time. They thought that the ship would pass them by but it changed course and headed towards them. Eventually it came close enough for Ben to distinguish the name, the Pasco.

Chapter 11
The Pasco

They were helped aboard the Pasco and were interested to see that the galleon sailed very low in the water. Obviously she was carrying some heavy cargo. Ben could tell The Professor was very excited and he soon found out the reason. They were ushered to the stern of the vessel and into the captain's cabin. It was luxuriously furnished and treasures of gold and gems decorated the sturdy furniture. In greeting the captain offered his hand.

"My name is Francis Drake," he said. Drake

was a handsome man, much weather beaten and his bright eyes pierced them, staring out of a deeply tanned face. He limped slightly as he moved from them, his injury causing him to wince. He sported a short beard and curly hair.

"I serve Her Majesty Queen Elizabeth," Drake continued, "and we are returning from great victory on the Spanish Main. Kindly tell me over a glass of ale, which is not of the best quality I'm afraid, but will refresh your obviously dry throats, how you come to be adrift so far from land in an open boat. Why are you here?"

"Because you picked us up," Ben replied, a little flippantly.

"Not a good answer!" Drake snapped, his manner suddenly changing so that Ben and the others feared things may develop into unpleasant consequences. This story book hero was after all really no more than a legalised pirate himself, used to plundering in the name of the Queen. Motioning for Ben to remain silent The Professor took up the story they had planned to tell any ship's captain who would fish them out of the sea. They had decided that any mention of pirates would be dangerous, especially as their mission was to kill the very man who now stood before them rightly demanding an account of their predicament.

"We were sailing on the Solway. We put out of Plymouth four weeks ago on a trading expedition. The crew mutinied and our Captain Mortimer was turned off the ship. We were loyal to him and so we suffered the same fate. This was a week ago. Our captain sadly died of a wound two days ago and we buried him at sea. I am James Brent and this here is Ben. Mabu is deaf and dumb so he won't be able to speak for himself. We are most grateful, Captain Drake, for your assistance and we are of course prepared to work our passage back to England. We too are loyal subjects of Her Majesty Queen Elizabeth."

Drake thought for a moment, stroking his

short beard. "As you have no doubt observed I am short of crew and extra hands are most welcome. We are carrying Spanish gold and gems we have plundered from Nombre de Dios. It will swell the coffers in Her Majesty's palace. I warn you now if you so much as touch any of our cargo you will swing from the yardarm. Do I make myself clear?"

They immediately stated that he had made himself perfectly clear.

"This has been a long voyage," he continued. "We set sail from Plymouth on 24th May 1572, so we have been away from our kingdom for over a year. I expect to reach Plymouth in two weeks at the latest, where you will be turned off. Good day."

The interview ended abruptly with Drake turning his back on them and studying a chart laid out on the table. A crewman showed them out and gave them a hammock each below decks. Ben was appalled at the squalor. There was a foul stench in the air that stuck in the back of his throat. Rats ran freely around and he did not look forward to the two weeks in these conditions. But he was a living part of history, he was aboard Francis Drake's ship. The Professor explained to him that they were sailing on the Pasco, which raided the Spanish colonies bringing back huge amounts of gold from Nombre de Dios. Drake's brother John had set out commanding the Swan, a smaller galleon, but he had been killed on the voyage. Drake had returned to Plymouth and after this he had sailed around the world in his new ship the Golden Hind, and later he fought the Spanish Armada, a story Ben vaguely knew.

The two weeks were the most interesting in Ben's life. He couldn't quite take it in that he was sailing in a galleon commanded by Sir Frances Drake. He felt again that it was all a dream and that he would soon wake up. He pinched himself to make sure he was awake. He was a living part of the past with the wise Professor as his friend, and together there was the hope that they may one day return to their own time and tell the greatest story in the world, but how and when?

On Sunday 9th August 1573, they docked at Plymouth. Crowds of onlookers lined the shoreline, giving Drake a hero's welcome. Mabu stood on the fo'c'sle waving and smiling. He had greatly impressed Drake with his hard and honest work and he was to stay with the ship's company where he had made some good friends.

A boat ferried the crew ashore. There were bands playing and food and drink for all. They went to an inn for a feast and there they thanked Drake for his help. The next morning after a hearty breakfast they bid him farewell, as Drake had to leave for London. Mabu escorted them to the door and Ben was truly saddened to leave his friend, but he was pleased that at last he would be treated well. With a fond embrace, they left Mabu standing at the doorway waving. As Ben and The Professor walked away they did not see the tears in Mabu's eyes.

They boarded a coach bound for Dartmouth

and as it drew away from the quayside another ship appeared on the horizon. The ship had been taken from the Spaniards at Nombre de Dios and after one week at sea it had also picked up a castaway who had survived at sea by floating on a piece of wreckage from the Black Albatross. Below decks all hands were busy at their duties. In one hammock lay the sole survivor of the pirate ship, the pirate who had vowed never to rest until he recovered the ruby he had stolen, and then lost in an instant. The talk aboard the ship was of 'the Pasco' which was half a day ahead of them and could be seen on the horizon. The Pasco had signalled three survivors had been rescued from a wrecked ship: two men and a boy. On hearing this news Bonecrusher Jake's thoughts grew more vengeful and murderous with every passing moment as they drew closer to land.

Chapter 12
Travellers on the road

The coach rattled on down the road to Dartmouth and soon Plymouth was lost from sight. Ben and The Professor were unable to discuss much of their peculiar adventure as there was a third occupant in the coach. He was a tailor returning to Devon after a business trip to Bath. Ben and The Professor found him to be a witty and very likeable travelling companion. It was wonderful to hear at first hand the experiences of a working man living in everyday Elizabethan England, and to discuss the various fashions of the day. Ben had shed his old weather stained clothes on the Pasco, and he was now well dressed in a smart red suit with lacy cuffs and collar paid for with the money James had brought with him from his time on the Pasco. The tailor commented favourably on his appearance.

Soon however the conversation ceased as the tailor nodded off, rocked to sleep by the motion of the coach. Ben and The Professor both enjoyed the experience of being back on dry land after so long as sea, even if the journey was going to be a long and uncomfortable one.

They passed through beautiful countryside unspoilt by mechanisation and roads. Ben marvelled at the peacefulness of the rolling hills and meadows, the unspoilt woodland and the open space. He wondered in his own mind if things had really changed for better since the 16th century. He decided that life was certainly easier in the 21st century but some simple pleasures of a slower pace of life had been lost through technological progress.

They stopped at a coaching station where

the horses were changed and they could enjoy the hospitality of the inn. The landlord, a stout jolly fellow, brought them bread, ham and fine ale and they spent a happy hour or two eating, drinking and recovering from the bumpy journey. They boarded the coach again for the afternoon run and the driver said he expected to reach their destination by nightfall. He was true to his word and in the twilight they drew up at another inn for their night's stopover.

As they slept, a horse bearing a weary figure clattered sweating and steaming into the courtyard. The figure dismounted shrouded in a black weather-stained cape, and like a shadow in the blackness he strode to the front door and rapped upon it. The startled, half-asleep landlord was complaining as he opened the door. He was not enthusiastic about offering hospitality to this burly wayfarer at such a late hour. The visitor's eyes appeared to be sinister and his face was hard as he demanded refreshment and a bed for the night. The landlord needed the money for the room so he complied with the stranger's request. Closing the bedroom door Bonecrusher Jake smiled as he removed his black cape, he had gained access to the inn where his quarry lay. After setting foot ashore at Plymouth half a day after the arrival of Drake's ship, he had extracted information about the arrival of The Professor and Ben from the captain of the port. He had followed the coach day and night, relentlessly pursuing his prey and with each mile of the journey his thoughts had become more bitter and his intentions more evil. The pirate knew better than to tackle his quarry in the crowded inn. He had dreamed of revenge and the ruby that he would take from them. He would bide his time and wait until they we well out into the countryside far from help. He sharpened and polished his cutlass late into the night and fell into a plotting sleep.

Chapter 13
Strange visitors

As the coach clattered over the cobbles of the courtyard with Ben and James the only occupants, they could hardly contain their excitement. They had held long discussions about the best course of action. Ben of course had wanted to go back to Seaford to try and recover the Time Globe from the beach where he had found it, but The Professor pointed out that it was probable that the Time Globe would not be found there. He believed that by the strange processes of time and fate the globe would be in the cave where he had originally found it, hidden in the rock face. At least that is what he reasoned as most likely. If they were to find the globe at all, the cave was the best place to look. Both of them were aware of course that the Time Globe may not be there at all, but this was their only hope. If the globe couldn't be found in the cave they agreed to look next in Seaford, and if that proved fruitless Ben and The Professor were resolved to stay stranded in time, leading the quiet lives of recluses until they both should die and be released from time for ever. Neither could risk becoming involved in the events of history for fear of changing history in some way.

Although they never again talked of this possibility it lurked in the back of both their minds as they travelled on to the place just south of Dartmouth, where The Professor had discovered the globe. They should easily find the caves as they lay just below a church which stood on the cliffs. After some hours James called to the driver to halt. The coach stopped and the driver called down that they were some

20 miles from Dartmouth. From the coach, James could see the small church protruding from the cliffs, and to the best of his knowledge he believed this was the place they had come through so many adventures to find once more.

They thanked the driver and, paying him handsomely for his trouble, they got out of the coach. The coach turned around, and with a cheery wave the driver drove back up the road. Later he would meet a lone horseman coming in the opposite direction who would further reward him for information as to the whereabouts of his two passengers.

With hearts beating in anticipation Ben and The Professor made their way to the old church. As they entered the churchyard James let out a whoop of delight.

"It is journey's end for us Ben!" he exclaimed. "This is it, this is the church I remember!" They followed the path around the church and down the cliffs, both of them breathless with the thrill of discovery. Scrambling down over rocks and stones they reached the shore. James carried on and as they passed the corner of the headland there was a dark opening in the cliff.

"Here is the cave Ben I'm sure of it." They looked at one another in hope and uncertainty. Ben followed The Professor into the darkness.

Any hopes they had of finding the globe dissolved with every step they took. It was pitch black in the cave and James suddenly let out a cry of pain as his head hit a rock.

"How stupid of me not to take account of this," he said. "We should have brought a lamp or candles. We'll do no good here without a light to work by."

"Candles will be no problem Professor," Ben replied. "All we have to do is pop into the church, surely we will find candles there."

They scrambled out of the cave and back up the cliff. Approaching the church they feared it may be locked but the door opened to the two strange visitors. As they closed the door behind them a figure rode silently up to the churchyard, the weather-beaten cloak drawn around him concealing a sharp and shining cutlass.

The church was small and simply furnished. Above the altar a simple window let in the glow of the morning sun. On it stood a cross and two candles – the objects of their visit. It was quiet but Ben and James sensed here a peace, as though all of time stood still in this old and holy place. Without speaking a word they both knelt before the altar and silently prayed for guidance. Never had the church received such strange visitors. Ben looked at the cross; it was the Christian symbol for over two thousand years. He had heard the story of Jesus at his church and school and he thought of his friends and family. Would he ever see them again? Then he saw it! A globe the size of a tennis ball set in the centre of the metal cross standing on the altar.

"James," he exclaimed, "It's the Time Globe; it's set into the cross, look!"

But James was looking behind him. He sensed Bonecrusher Jake's entry into the church even though the door had opened silently.

"You bilge rats!" the pirate shouted. "Prepare

to meet your maker!" He drew his cutlass advancing down the aisle. "Give me my ruby!" he snarled.

"Quick Ben!" cried The Professor. "Hold up the cross to the window and the setting sun's rays and I'll hold him off."

Ben hesitated for seconds but obeyed The Professor. He leapt to the altar and holding up the cross caught the sun's rays in the globe. He experienced the swirling colours around him and he began to spin in time catching glimpses of The Professor and Bonecrusher Jake wrestling together as if in a mist. The Pirate's hands had The Professor's head in a vice like grip - and then he saw nothing.

Chapter 14
Summer ends

"Ben are you alright?"

He opened his eyes and stared up at his own familiar ceiling in his own familiar room. His mother and father sat beside his bed. The seagulls rasped their hungry sounds and outside someone was mowing a lawn.

"What year is this?" He raised himself onto one elbow and saw his own clothes, the ones he put on that morning, folded on his chair.

"That's a strange question to ask son," replied his father.

"What date is it today?" Ben insisted.

"The 27th July" replied his father, "How do you feel?"

"Have I been dreaming?" Ben murmured. "How did I get here?"

His mother explained how he had been found wandering on the beach by Mr Wylie, their neighbour, and how he had been brought home muttering about someone called Bonecrusher Jake. Over and over again he had repeated the name and then he had fallen asleep. The doctor had been called and Ben seemed to be well, apart from obvious exhaustion. The doctor had told them to call if Ben appeared to get worse but he put his condition down to the flu virus which had been around during the summer.

Ben began to tell them about the Time Globe and his adventures with the pirates. His parents listened and looked at him slightly concerned, and then almost amused.

"What an imagination you have," his mother said, patting his arm. Ben was going to argue with them but suddenly realized it was going to be hopeless, perhaps he had dreamed it all.

"I'm starving," he said, "Is there anything to eat?"

His mother smiled. "Dinner's ready," she replied as she winked at Ben. "There are some cakes waiting to be eaten."

The final days of the summer holiday Ben spent playing and combing the beach just in case there might be a clear globe about the size of a tennis ball lying anywhere. Surrounded now by his family and friends and returning to his old routines the memories of his adventures began to fade, and he thought about the new school year and a new teacher, Mr Wall, into whose class he had thankfully been put. Miss Proud had left during the Summer to teach in Africa as a Missionary. He had thought she was dull. How wrong he had been! Soon the first day of term arrived and he set off to school looking forward to a new classroom and new things to learn.

He was seated near the front of the classroom next to Colin Wilkins, his best friend. Mr Wall explained to the class the work they would be doing in the first term: Maths, English and of course a science project. This year they would be finding out about the earth and Mr Wall had prepared some interesting things for them to do. They were to visit museums, have some visiting speakers and watch a TV series for schools called 'Our World'. They were to watch the first programme that afternoon and Ben could hardly wait, it was all about how the earth began and how rocks were formed. They would see volcanoes and perhaps even dinosaurs.

The afternoon came quickly and the class were all sitting in front of the interactive whiteboard. Mr Wall introduced the programme and they all sat quietly, apart from Colin who was told off for pinching Allison Smith's bottom and had to sit next to Mr Evans the teaching assistant.

"Years ago," the narrator's voice spoke smoothly from the screen, "the earth was a huge mass of molten rock spinning in space and time. As it cooled, so different rocks were formed. Many of them are now buried deeply within the earth and some are very precious. We now hear from Professor James Brent of Southampton University."

Ben stared astonished as The Professor's face appeared on the screen. He looked slightly older; he had acquired a few more grey hairs and a scar above his right eye. He spoke with the same quiet voice, as he held up precious stones and talked about them, how they were formed and how they were discovered. As he held the large ruby up to the camera Ben finally knew that his adventures had all been true, that it had all actually happened! He would go and visit Professor Brent one day soon.

The TV programme ended and the class were dismissed. Ben spent the rest of the day in deep thought. That night Ben wrote a letter.

Dear Professor Brent,

I saw you on TV today. I saw the ruby. I see you now have a scar. I expect it may have come from a certain villainous pirate. May I come and see you?

Your friend for all time,

Ben

He addressed the envelope:

Professor James Brent,
Geology Department,
Southampton University,
Hampshire

Three days later the letter arrived in the in-tray on Professor Brent's desk. He opened it and he laughed as he read it. He had puzzled about Ben's whereabouts. But having returned to 1999, Ben was not yet born. Over the years, other things had gained importance and the memories became dreams. Now it was the right time. They would have to get together and talk about the whole thing. They might even have discovered something new together which would have been of use to others in this time. He walked over to the wall facing the window. Behind a painting of a Lakeland scene was a small safe. He opened it and smiled. In amongst the collection of gem stones lay a crystal clear globe about the size of a tennis ball.

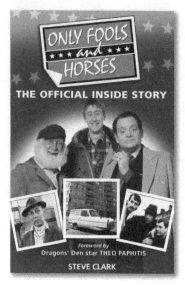

Only Fools and Horses - The Official Inside Story
By Steve Clark
Foreword by Theo Paphitis

This book takes us behind the scenes to reveal the secrets of the hit show and is fully authorised by the family of its writer John Sullivan.

This engaging tribute contains interviews with the show's stars and members of the production team, together with rarely seen pictures.

Written by bestselling author Steve Clark, the only writer on set for the filming of *Only Fools and Horses*, *The Green Green Grass* and *Rock & Chips*, this book gives a fascinating and unique insight into this legendary series.
£9.99 (paperback)

The Official Only Fools and Horses Quiz Book
Compiled by Dan Sullivan and Jim Sullivan,
Foreword by John Sullivan

Now you can test your knowledge of the legendary sitcom in *The Official Only Fools and Horses Quiz Book*, which is packed with more than 1,000 brain-teasers about the show.

Plus there's an episode guide and an exclusive foreword by the show's creator and writer John Sullivan, who reveals some of the mystery behind the much-loved series and just how he came up with some of television's most memorable moments.
£7.99 (paperback)